CAT'S CRADLE

LUCY DANIELS
Cat's Cradle

Illustrated by Paul Howard

Hodder
Children's
Books

a division of Hodder Headline Limited

Special thanks to Sue Welford

Animal Ark Pets is registered trademark of Working Partners Limited
Text copyright © 1999 Working Partners Limited
Created by Working Partners Limited, London W12 7QY
Original series created by Ben M. Baglio
Illustrations copyright © 1999 Paul Howard
Cover illustration by Chris Chapman

First published in Great Britain in 1999
by Hodder Children's Books

A Catalogue record for this book is available from the British Library

ISBN 0 340 73592 9

Typeset by Avon Dataset Ltd, Bidford-on-Avon, Warks

Printed and bound in Great Britain by
The Guernsey Press Co. Ltd, Channel Islands

Hodder Children's Books
a division of Hodder Headline Limited
338 Euston Road
London NW1 3BH

Contents

Contents

1

A Christmas orphan

"I've got a brilliant idea, Mrs Todd!" Mandy Hope announced excitedly when it was her turn to speak. She'd been holding up her hand to get her teacher's attention for what seemed like ages!

There were two weeks to go before school broke up for Christmas. Mandy's class were talking about the juniors' Christmas pageant, which was to be presented after the infants' nativity play on the last day of term. It was called "Christmas Through the Ages", and all the juniors were going to dress up in all sorts of costumes – from Roman times right through to the present day.

Mrs Todd smiled. "Right, Mandy," she said. "Let's hear it."

Mandy felt a tingle of anticipation as she stood up. "Well, I was thinking . . ." she began. "Why don't we have *animals* in the pageant as well? It would make it much more interesting!"

Mandy loved animals. Her parents had a veterinary surgery called Animal Ark in Welford, the Yorkshire village where they all lived. The family's stone cottage was attached to the surgery, which meant that Mandy got to meet all Animal Ark's patients.

"Does that mean you want to dress up in a donkey costume again?" Mrs Todd asked, laughing.

Mandy laughed too. When she was in the infants she had wanted to play a donkey in the stable with Mary and Joseph, not an angel round the crib. She shook her head. "No, *real* animals this time, Mrs Todd!"

"Real ones?" Mandy's class teacher looked a bit surprised.

"Yes," Mandy replied. "I mean, there were lots of animals in the stable when baby Jesus was born, weren't there?"

Mrs Todd nodded. "Yes, there were, Mandy," she said. "But we couldn't have real cows or donkeys on the stage. They would be far too big."

Everyone laughed at the thought of farm animals tramping on to the stage in the school hall.

"No, of course not." Mandy giggled. "But why couldn't we have smaller animals like cats and dogs – and maybe other pets, too?"

Mrs Todd looked thoughtful. "They would have to be very well-behaved," she began.

"There might have been a guinea-pig in the stable when Jesus was born," Pam Stanton piped up. "I could bring Ginny. She's always very good."

Everyone began talking excitedly and Mrs Todd had to clap her hands for silence. "Settle down, now," she called. "Miss Oswald is organising the celebrations this year. I'll have to talk to *her* about Mandy's idea." Miss Oswald was Class 1's teacher. "I'll let you know what she says."

Mandy sat down, feeling hopeful. Her mind was in a whirl. It would be really special if everyone could bring their pets to be in the pageant. Mandy didn't have a pet, but she loved getting to know all her friends' animals. Her mum and dad were always so busy looking after other people's pets that there just wasn't time for the Hopes to have one of their own.

When school was over for the day, Mandy waited by the gate for her best friend, James Hunter. She and James always walked home together. Mandy couldn't wait to tell him about her idea for the pageant.

James was a year younger than Mandy and in Class 4. He lived on the other side of the village green and had a Labrador puppy called Blackie and a cat named Benji. James loved animals almost as much as Mandy did.

"Real pets! Wow! That would be great!" James exclaimed when she told him. "I could bring Blackie!"

As much as Mandy loved Blackie, she wasn't sure *that* was such a good idea. Blackie was the nicest puppy in the world, but he certainly wasn't the most well-behaved. "We'll have to wait and see what Miss Oswald says," she said hurriedly. She didn't want to hurt James's feelings by saying that Blackie might cause trouble.

When they reached the village green, Mandy and James went their separate ways home. Mandy waved goodbye, then hurried off. It was snowing lightly and there was a thin covering of white on the ground. She wrapped her bright woolly scarf tighter round her neck as she skidded along the lane to Animal Ark. She felt excited all over again. If there was a *lot* of snow, she and James might be able to go tobogganing at the weekend. That would be brilliant fun.

When Mandy ran in through the back door bursting with news, her mum was in the kitchen, getting tea ready. Mandy stamped the snow from her shoes on the doormat and blew on her fingers to warm them up.

"So, it's still snowing," Mrs Hope said, smiling at Mandy's glowing face.

"Just a bit," Mandy said. "And it's freezing cold."

"I'll make you a mug of hot chocolate," her mum said. "That's a sure cure for cold fingers and toes."

"Great!" Mandy stood warming herself by

the stove as she told her mum about plans for the nativity play and pageant.

"It sounds really good," Mrs Hope said, putting a steaming mug of hot chocolate on the table and fetching a bag of crisps from the cupboard. Mandy was always hungry when she got home from school.

"Thanks, Mum," Mandy said, taking a sip of her drink and tearing open the bag of crisps. "And I've asked Mrs Todd if real animals can take part," she gabbled excitedly. "Small ones, of course. Not ponies or cows or anything. Don't you think that would be brilliant? She's going to ask Miss Oswald!"

"It would be lovely," Mrs Hope replied. "But don't get too excited, Mandy, because Miss Oswald may not think it's a good idea."

"*What* might not be a good idea?" Mandy's dad, Adam Hope, came through from the surgery.

Mandy repeated her idea for the Christmas pageant.

Mr Hope chuckled as he poured himself a hot chocolate from the pan. "Well, I think that sounds fantastic, Mandy."

Mandy grinned at her dad, who came to join them at the kitchen table.

A few minutes later, there was an urgent knocking at the back door. The cold wind blew a flurry of snowflakes into the room as Mandy hurried to open it. To her surprise, Miss Oswald was standing on the doorstep looking cold and very upset about something.

Miss Oswald was a tall, thin woman. She wore glasses and had rather a stern-looking face, even though she was very gentle and kind when you got to know her.

"Hello, Miss Oswald!" Mandy exclaimed, surprised to see the teacher standing there. "Come in." She stood back to let her into the kitchen.

"I'm so sorry to bother you," Miss Oswald said quickly to Mr and Mrs Hope. "I went round to the surgery door, but it wasn't open."

"Evening surgery starts in half an hour," Emily Hope informed her. "But don't worry. Come in and stand by the stove and get warm.

You look frozen."

Mandy suddenly noticed that Miss Oswald was cradling something inside her thick winter coat. "What have you got in there?" she asked curiously.

The teacher carefully drew out a bedraggled, young black cat. Mandy gasped. The cat gave a faint miaow and stared at her with big, frightened eyes. It cowered against Miss Oswald, obviously scared to death.

Miss Oswald held the cat close, her face softening as she gently stroked it. "I found it hiding in my garage when I got back from school," she explained. "I've only just got home because we've been discussing plans for the Christmas show. I don't know how long the poor thing's been there, but it was shivering with cold and it's very thin," she said worriedly.

She gazed at the Hopes, her eyes bright with tears behind her glasses. "Would you take a look at it for me? It can hardly stand up and I'm worried it's been injured in some way."

Mandy reached out and touched the cat's straggly fur as Miss Oswald handed the little

creature to Mrs Hope. Her heart turned over as she saw how thin and nervous the cat was. She wondered why it was hiding in Miss Oswald's garage on such a cold winter's night. Mandy couldn't bear to think how confused and frightened it must have felt, hiding alone in the dark.

"Poor scrap," Mr Hope said. The cat miaowed weakly again.

"Let's take it through to the surgery," Mrs Hope suggested. "We can give it a thorough examination there."

"Can I come?" Mandy asked hopefully.

Mr Hope nodded as he opened the door for Miss Oswald and Mrs Hope to go through.

"Mum and Dad are looking after a sick snake at the moment." Mandy chattered away to Miss Oswald as she went with them into the surgery.

"A snake?" Miss Oswald repeated. She looked startled.

"Don't worry, it's quite a harmless one." Mr Hope grinned. "And anyway, it's tucked up safely for the night."

In the surgery Mandy's mum gave the young

cat a thorough examination. "Well, she's a female," Mrs Hope said. Then she looked at the cat's eyes and ears, and examined her mouth and teeth before running her hands down the cat's spine and over her legs. "There's nothing broken," she announced at last. She took her stethoscope and listened to the cat's heartbeat. "And her heart and lungs sound OK."

Mandy let out a sigh of relief.

"I was scared she'd been hit by a car," Miss Oswald said, still gazing anxiously at the little creature, "even though I couldn't find any obvious injuries on her."

"No, there aren't any," Mrs Hope confirmed, putting her stethoscope away. She gently pulled up the skin on the back of the cat's neck. The skin stayed up in a hump for a moment or two before going back into place. "But she is dehydrated; she needs a drink – and she's weak from lack of food."

"I tried giving her some milk," Miss Oswald said. "But it made her sick."

"In that case," said Mr Hope, "we'd better keep her here for a day or two to keep an eye on her. She could have picked up an infection."

"We'll just try her with a little more milk then, and see what happens," Mrs Hope added. "If she doesn't keep it down, she'll need to be fed straight into her veins with a glucose drip." She went into the kitchen to heat up a saucer of milk.

"We'll keep her in the back room. That's where sick animals are kept overnight," Mr Hope explained to Miss Oswald, as he carried the little cat through to the residential unit. Mrs Hope followed a couple of minutes later with a saucer of milk.

Soon the little stray was settled into a large, wire cat cage with a soft blanket underneath her. She was curled up, looking at them with her large green eyes.

Mrs Hope placed the saucer of milk inside the cage, together with a dish of water. She closed the door gently. "There," she said softly. "We'll pop back later to see if she's drunk any milk and if she's managed to keep it down."

"I wonder where she came from," Mandy

said as they tiptoed away.

"I've no idea," Miss Oswald said. "But I'll ask around my neighbours when I get home. Someone is missing her, I'm sure."

"Yes, they're bound to be," Mrs Hope said when they were back in the kitchen. "She's such a sweet little thing. But she could have wandered a long way from home. It looks like she's been living outside for quite a while."

Miss Oswald sighed and turned to look at Mandy. "She reminds me of a cat I had when I was about your age. Her name was Tinker."

"That's a nice name," Mandy said. "Shall we call her that until we find out what her real name is?"

"Yes, that's a nice idea," Miss Oswald said with a smile.

"I'm afraid we won't be able to keep her here once she's recovered," Mandy's dad warned the teacher as they went to the front door with her. "If her owner doesn't turn up, would *you* be able to keep her?"

Mandy crossed her fingers and really hoped Miss Oswald would say yes. She knew that the teacher lived in a house all by herself. A little cat would be great company for her.

But Miss Oswald shook her head sadly. "I'd love to," she said. "But I'm out all day at school. It wouldn't be fair to leave such a nervous little cat on her own for such a long time every day."

Mr Hope nodded. "You're right. Until Tinker's fully recovered from her ordeal, it would be better if she wasn't left on her own." He sighed. "It looks as if we might have to ask Betty Hilder at the animal sanctuary to take her, then." Betty lived just outside of the village and ran a rescue centre for stray and unwanted animals.

The teacher said goodbye to them, then went down the path and got into her car.

As she watched Miss Oswald drive away, Mandy sighed. "Tinker looks so sad," she said unhappily. "And so does Miss Oswald. If Tinker isn't claimed, it would be so nice if she could have her as a pet."

Mandy's dad gave her a hug. "Yes, Mandy, it would, but as Miss Oswald has to be at school

15

all day, I'm afraid it just isn't possible."

Later that evening, before she went to bed, Mandy couldn't resist going back to take a peep at Tinker. She was still curled up on the blanket and was fast asleep now. Mandy's dad had already been back to check that she hadn't been sick again and he'd told her that Tinker had managed to keep a small amount of milk down.

"Are you feeling better?" Mandy murmured. She felt full of concern for the pretty little cat.

Fancy not having a warm and cosy home to live in! Especially at Christmas, when it should be such a happy time for people *and* pets.

Mandy put her finger through the wire and gently touched Tinker's soft fur. It was warm and fluffy, now that she had dried out. She was breathing with little soft rumbles as if she was purring in her sleep.

Mrs Hope came in and put her hand on Mandy's shoulder. "Don't worry, love," she said. "If her owner doesn't turn up, Betty will find her a nice new home, I'm sure."

But Mandy couldn't help worrying. Supposing no one claimed Tinker and Betty *couldn't* find her a nice home? Then what would happen?

2

Plans

"And poor Tinker looked so thin and frightened," Mandy said sadly to James as they walked to school the following morning. "It's awful that she's homeless at Christmas time."

"We'll have to ask everyone at school if they've lost a cat," James said, rubbing his hands together. Even though he was wearing thick woolly gloves and a scarf, he looked cold and his nose was bright red. It was a bitter day. The sky was grey and cloudy and it looked like more snow was on the way.

"Definitely," Mandy agreed. "Anyway, she did seem a lot better this morning when I went to see her. Mum and Dad are still going to keep her in the residential unit for a few days, though, so they can keep an eye on her."

"Then what will happen to her?" James asked as they went through the school gates, slipping and skidding across the frozen playground.

Mandy explained about her dad asking Betty Hilder to have Tinker at the sanctuary. "But she won't go there until Mum and Dad are sure she's OK," she added.

James looked thoughtful. "Why can't Miss Oswald keep her?"

Mandy told him what the teacher had said about looking after Tinker.

"Oh, poor cat," James said sadly. "I hope her owners turn up."

"Yes," Mandy said. "Me too."

The bell went for everyone to line up. When

Mandy got to her classroom she grabbed some paper and pencils and quickly made a notice about Tinker for the school bulletin board. She just had time to pin it up before lining up to go into the hall for assembly.

Mandy was still thinking about Tinker in assembly, when she suddenly heard the Headteacher, Mrs Garvie, say her name.

"Mandy Hope has suggested we have real pets in the pageant," Mrs Garvie said, looking over in Mandy's direction. "And both Miss Oswald and I have agreed that it's a splendid idea."

Mandy's heart gave a flutter as everyone began whispering to each other excitedly.

"We'll be holding pet auditions at the beginning of next week," Mrs Garvie continued. "Miss Oswald will be in charge of the auditions. If you want to bring your pet, go and see her so she can add your name to the list."

James's class sat in front of Mandy's. He turned round to whisper to her. "I'd like to enter Blackie," he said. "Of course, I'd have to keep my fingers crossed that he'd behave himself."

"Yes," she said, smiling at her friend. "You would!"

After assembly, Mrs Todd had another announcement to make to Mandy's class. She read out a list of the parts that everyone was to play in the "Christmas Through the Ages" pageant.

Mandy held her breath with excitement as her teacher went down the list.

"Gary Roberts," Mrs Todd said. "You're to be a peasant boy from the sixteenth century."

"A peasant boy!" Gary said. "What will I need to wear?"

"A tunic made out of brown material," Mrs Todd said. "And leggings."

"Leggings!" Gary pulled a face and began talking to the girl sitting next to him.

"Sarah," Mrs Todd called out the name of another of Mandy's friends. "You are to come as a girl who lived in ancient Roman times."

Mandy had to wait a long time to hear her own name.

Finally, Mrs Todd said, "Mandy, you're to be dressed as a girl who lived when Queen Victoria was on the throne."

"I wonder what kind of a dress I'll need for that," Mandy whispered excitedly to her friend Richard Tanner.

"No idea," he answered. Richard was going to be dressed in clothes that young people wore in the 1970s.

To help them with their costumes, Mrs Todd showed them a history book from the school library. The book had been chosen at the school book fair and bought with money raised at the summer Fun Day. It had lots of pictures of young people's clothes through the ages in it.

"Get on with your reading," she told them, "and I'll call you up one by one to show you a picture of the kind of costume you'll need to wear for the pageant."

When Mandy's turn came, Mrs Todd showed her a picture of a Victorian girl dressed in a long, crinoline dress with lots of petticoats. "It's lovely," Mandy gasped. "But where am I going to get a dress like that?"

Mandy was still wondering about this when she went back to her desk and sat down. Suddenly she had an idea. Her gran was good at dressmaking – she would go over to Lilac Cottage and ask her if she would help to make her costume.

When breaktime came, Mandy spotted James in the playground and hurried across to talk to him.

"I've asked everyone in my class if they know anyone who's lost a cat," James told her. "But no one does."

Mandy sighed. "I made a notice for the bulletin board. Let's hope someone gets in touch."

They went on to talk about their parts in the pageant.

"I've got to dress as a boy from the second world war," James said. "I've seen a picture in a history book, but I'm not sure where my mum's going to get the clothes from."

"I'm going to ask Gran if she'll help me with my costume," Mandy said. "I bet she'll help you with yours, too. Let's go and see her after school, shall we?"

"Good idea," James agreed.

After school, Mandy and James hurried back to Animal Ark to visit Tinker before they went on to see Mandy's gran and grandad.

The little black cat *was* looking brighter, but she still seemed very weak and was a bit nervous of them at first.

Mr Hope allowed them to take Tinker gently from her cage to give her a cuddle. "She's really sweet," James said. "It's a shame Miss Oswald can't keep her. She'd make such a lovely pet."

"She would," Mr Hope said. "And Miss Oswald already seems rather fond of her."

James phoned his mum to let her know he was going to be late coming home from school. Then he and Mandy told Mr Hope about the plans for the pageant.

"And we're going to ask Gran to help us with the costumes," Mandy added.

"It sounds as if it's going to be great," Mr Hope said as they put Tinker gently back into her cage. "I'll look forward to seeing the two of you dressed up."

Mandy and James were just leaving for Lilac Cottage when they saw Miss Oswald coming down the path.

"I've been thinking about Tinker all day," Miss Oswald admitted, as Mandy took her through to see the little cat. "How is she today?"

"A bit better," Mandy said.

There were tears in the teacher's eyes as she cuddled the little cat. "You know, she is *so* like my own dear Tinker," she told Mandy and James. "I've never stopped missing her."

"Did she get lost, too?" James asked.

"Oh, no," Miss Oswald said. "She died, I'm afraid. But she was very old – almost eighteen."

"Eighteen!" James exclaimed. "That's *really* old for a cat."

Miss Oswald nodded and held Tinker even closer to her. The cat purred, rubbing her face against the sleeve of her coat. She clearly liked being with Miss Oswald.

Mr Hope was watching from the doorway.

"Thank you so much for keeping an eye on her, Mr Hope," Miss Oswald said gratefully.

"She hasn't been any bother at all," Mr Hope assured her. "And she should be fit enough to go to the sanctuary in a day or two."

Miss Oswald bit her lip. "I hope she'll be well looked after there."

"Oh, she will, honestly," Mandy piped up. "Betty Hilder loves animals and she's great with them."

"I'll let you know when I'm taking her, so you can come and say goodbye to her before I leave," Mr Hope said kindly.

"Thank you," Miss Oswald said, giving Tinker one last cuddle before putting her gently back in her cage. She seemed very sad to be leaving the little cat again.

It was already getting dark, and the light from the street lamps gave an orange glow to the sprinkling of snow on the ground as Mandy and James set off for Lilac Cottage. Mandy had rung her grandparents to let them know they were coming.

They had just reached the end of the lane when they met Mrs Hope driving towards them in the Animal Ark Land-rover. She drew up beside them and wound down the window. "Where are you two off to?" she asked, her green eyes twinkling.

"We're going to Gran's," Mandy replied. She quickly told her mum about their parts in the pageant.

"That's great news," Mrs Hope said. "Well, you're going to visit just the right person. Gran's really clever with her sewing-machine."

When Mandy and James reached Lilac Cottage, Mandy's gran was in the kitchen. She looked up and smiled as they walked in through the back door. "Hello, you two!" A delicious smell of mince pies wafted out from under a teacloth on the kitchen table.

Gran saw James eyeing it hungrily. She lifted the cloth. "Help yourself," she said, smiling. "But mind you don't burn your mouth – they're still a bit hot."

"Great! Thanks," James said, as he took one off the cooling tray and sat down at the table.

Gran poured out two glasses of milk and brought them over.

"Thanks, Gran," Mandy said. She unwound her scarf, helped herself to a mince pie and sat down beside James.

Grandad came through into the kitchen. He sniffed the air. "Hmm, I thought I could smell mince pies." He popped one on a plate and pulled up a chair next to Mandy. "Nice to see the two of you. How are you both?"

Gran gazed at Mandy. "You look a bit upset, love. What's wrong?" She could always tell when something was troubling Mandy.

"It's Tinker," Mandy said unhappily.

"Tinker?" Gran looked puzzled, then Mandy told her all about the stray cat.

"Oh dear, poor thing," Gran said. "I'll ask around the village, shall I? *Someone* will know where she's come from, I'm sure."

"I'll spread the word up at the allotment, as well," Grandad said.

Gran and Grandad had lived in Welford all their lives and knew almost everybody in the village.

"Thanks," Mandy said gratefully. Then she explained the reason for their visit. "Actually, we've come to ask you a favour."

"That's a surprise!" her grandad teased her.

"That's what grandparents are for, Tom," Gran said, smiling. "All right then, fire away!"

Together, Mandy and James told them about the pageant and the costumes they needed.

"Would you be able to make me a Victorian dress, Gran?" Mandy asked. "Mrs Todd found a picture of one in a book that I could bring to show you."

"A Victorian dress," Gran repeated. "Well, that's quite a task. But there's no need for me to see a picture: I've got a good idea what Victorian dresses looked like." Then she turned to James, looking thoughtful. "A boy from the second world war . . ." she murmured. "Well then, James, you'll need short trousers, long socks up to your knees and a Fair Isle jumper."

"*Short* trousers?" James exclaimed, sounding horrified.

"That's right," Gran said with a smile. "That's

what boys wore in those days."

Mandy chuckled. "You'll look brilliant in short trousers, James."

"*Will* I?" James said, screwing up his nose. "I wonder where my mum could get a pair from?"

"Don't worry about that," Gran smiled. "I'll make you a pair. You tell your mum that she can leave it up to me, James."

"Thanks," James said. He didn't look at all sure he wanted to wear short trousers.

"And you'll need a gas mask," Grandad said.

"A *gas mask!*" Mandy shrieked. "What on earth for?"

"Well," Grandad said, handing around the mince pies, "during the Blitz, when bombs were being dropped on buildings, everyone had to carry a gas mask with them. Just in case any gas leaked out from damaged pipes where the bombs exploded."

"How did they carry them?" Mandy asked.

"In boxes. They had long straps that went round your neck," Grandad replied.

"It must have felt a bit strange having to carry

32

a gas mask with you all the time," Mandy said.

"We soon got used to it," Gran explained. "We knew a gas mask could save our lives if we needed to put it on. But I can't imagine where we'll find one for James."

Grandad folded his arms. "If James is going to look the part, then he'll *have* to have a gas mask," he insisted.

"When is this pageant of yours?" Gran asked.

"On the last day of term," James told her. "And we're having real animals in it."

"Real animals!" Grandad exclaimed. "That will be grand."

"The school's having pet auditions next week," Mandy piped up.

"Are you going to enter Blackie?" Gran asked James.

"I sure am!" James said. "Blackie hates to be left out of anything."

"Oh!" Gran winked at Mandy. "That *will* be fun, then."

"Well," Grandad said, "it sounds as if Welford Village School's Christmas show is going to be pretty special this year." Then he grinned at James. "And if Blackie passes his audition, I bet he'll be the star!"

James grinned back, his mouth full of his second mince pie. "Hope so," he said.

3
No room

After breakfast a couple of days later, Mandy went through to the surgery to see Tinker.

It was Saturday, the day Mr Hope was going to take the little stray cat up to Welford Animal Sanctuary. He had rung Betty the day before to make sure she had room for her.

Tinker was much better than when she had

arrived at Animal Ark, but she was still quite nervous and shy – except with Miss Oswald, whom she seemed to adore. Tinker was sitting up, daintily washing her face with her paws, when Mandy reached her cage.

Simon, the veterinary nurse, was in the residential unit. He was busy tidying up. "Have you come to see Tinker?" he asked.

Mandy nodded and gave a big sigh. "Dad's taking her to Betty Hilder's this morning." She opened the door of the cage and lifted the cat out. Then she went and sat on a chair with Tinker on her lap and began grooming her with a soft brush. "I'm really going to miss you," she told the little cat. Tinker gave a small miaow.

"I'm sure she'll miss you, as well," Simon said.

Just then, the door opened and Mr Hope came through, followed by Miss Oswald.

"I've come to say goodbye to Tinker," the teacher told Mandy and Simon. She took the cat gently from Mandy and gave her a cuddle. "Now, you be good at Betty's," she whispered

in Tinker's velvety ear. "And be happy in your new home."

Tinker purred loudly and rubbed her cheek against Miss Oswald's face.

Miss Oswald handed the little cat sadly to Mr Hope. She watched as he put Tinker into a pet carrier ready for her journey to the animal sanctuary.

"Are you *sure* you can't have her?" Mandy said. She didn't like to see Miss Oswald looking so sad, and had to ask just *once* more. "Isn't there anyone who might pop in to visit her while you're at work?"

"Now, Mandy," her dad said, "I'm sure Miss Oswald would have Tinker if it was at all possible."

Miss Oswald smiled kindly at Mandy. "No, I'm afraid I can't think of anyone."

"But it doesn't seem fair," Mandy protested. "You love each other so much."

Tears came into Miss Oswald's eyes again. "I know," she said.

"Never mind," Mandy said quickly, worried that she had upset the teacher. "I'm sure Betty will find someone who'll love her just as much as you do. She only lets her animals go to really good homes, you know."

Miss Oswald sighed. "I hope so, Mandy. I really do." She gave Tinker one last, sorrowful glance, then hurried out.

Mandy's dad looked thoughtful as he watched Miss Oswald. He shook his head. "I wish there was something we could do to help," he said.

"Me too," Mandy agreed.

Her dad gazed at her. "Do you want to come to the sanctuary with me?"

"Yes, please, Dad." Mandy loved going to Welford Animal Sanctuary to see all Betty's rescued animals, and she wanted to see Tinker settled in there.

Her dad put his arm round her and gave her a hug. "Never mind, love. I'm sure *someone* can give Tinker a good home."

Mandy knew her dad was right, but that didn't stop her feeling sad that Miss Oswald couldn't have Tinker.

They put the carrier in the back of the Land-rover and drove through the village, over the bridge and up the narrow, winding road that led to the animal sanctuary. The broad, snowy sweep of the Dales looked bright in the winter sunshine.

As they reached the gate, Mandy jumped out and rushed to open it. When her dad had driven through, she closed it again, then ran to knock on Betty's front door.

Dogs were barking and cats miaowing in their row of pens behind the bungalow. There were a few sheep in the field just behind and next to it a smaller field with goats in. All the animals at the sanctuary had been rescued from cruel owners or had been found abandoned. People brought them to Betty to be looked after.

There was no answer at the door, so Mandy called out to her dad. "Let's go and see if she's in the stable yard."

When they entered the yard, Betty was just coming out of one of the stables carrying a pitchfork. A shaggy Shetland pony was chomping fodder from a hay-net tied to one of the stable doors.

"Good morning, Betty," Mr Hope called.

"Morning, Adam," she replied. "Hello, Mandy. I see you've brought the little cat you phoned me about."

"Her name's Tinker," Mandy said.

Betty bent down and peered into the cat carrier that Mr Hope was holding, "She *is* a poor, sweet thing," she said. But then she shook her head. "I'm really sorry, Adam, someone brought two cats in late yesterday evening. They had both been terribly neglected

41

so I couldn't turn them away. They've taken the last cage, I'm afraid, so there's no room for this little one after all."

"Oh, dear," Mandy's dad said.

"I'm really sorry," Betty repeated. "I meant to phone you early this morning, but I've been rushed off my feet."

"But she's got nowhere else to go!" Mandy said worriedly.

Betty looked thoughtful. "Well, if that's really the case then I'll *have* to take her in. You know I never turn an animal away. But all my cat accommodation is full up, and you know what it will be like after Christmas – there'll be lots more abandoned pets." She took another look at Tinker. "The poor little thing looks scared stiff."

"She is," Mandy said. "We think she had a bad time before Miss Oswald found her."

Betty shook her head again. "In that case, she needs more attention than I'll be able to give her. I could have her in the house with me, but I've already got three cats in there, and she's so small I'm afraid they might bully her. Are you *sure* that no one else can take her?"

"Miss Oswald wants her," Mandy said sadly, "but she can't be at home all day to look after her."

Mr Hope was stroking his beard and looking thoughtful. "OK, Betty," he said suddenly, "we don't want to risk Tinker being bullied. Thanks anyway. I think it would be best if we take her back with us for now."

"You know, Dad," Mandy said, as they drove back down the hill towards Welford. "It's a bit like Joseph and Mary."

Her dad glanced at her. "What is?"

"Well, there not being enough room at the sanctuary for Tinker. There wasn't enough room for Joseph and Mary at the inn, either, was there?"

Her dad gave Mandy one of his lopsided grins. "No, there wasn't."

"But they found somewhere to stay in the end, didn't they?" Mandy continued.

"Yes," Mr Hope agreed. "Somewhere warm

and cosy. Maybe we'll find somewhere for Tinker, too, if we're lucky."

Mandy looked at her dad. There was something in his tone of voice that told her he was planning something. *And* he had an unmistakable twinkle in his eye! "What are you up to, Dad?" she asked curiously.

He tapped his nose and gave her a wink. "Wait and see," he said mysteriously.

As they passed Bleakfell Hall, a large house that stood a little way back from the road, Mandy's gran was just driving out of the gates. Mandy could see a bulging black plastic sack on the back seat of her car.

Mr Hope pulled up and wound down the car window. "Hi, Mum. What are you doing up here?"

"I've been sorting through the WI drama group's costumes," Gran explained. "Mrs Ponsonby keeps them in one of her spare rooms." She grinned at Mandy. "And I spotted something that would make a wonderful dress for you, Mandy. Come and see me later and I'll show you."

Saying goodbye, Gran wound up her window again and drove off before Mandy could ask more about her costume.

"Hmm," Mandy grumbled to herself. "*Everyone* is being mysterious today."

4

An early Christmas present

When they got back to Animal Ark, James and Blackie were standing by the front gate waiting for Mandy. "Do you fancy coming for a walk in Monkton Spinney with us?" James asked, as soon as Mandy got out of the Land-rover.

Monkton Spinney was a small wood just over

the bridge at the end of the village.

"I'd love to," Mandy said, bending down to give Blackie a hug. He jumped up and tried to lick her nose.

"Before you do that, could you just take Tinker back into the surgery and put her in one of the cages, please?" Mr Hope asked. He handed the pet carrier to Mandy, then hurried off, saying, "I've got an important phone call to make."

Blackie wasn't allowed in the residential unit, so they left him with Jean Knox, Animal Ark's receptionist.

"We won't be a minute," Mandy told her as James tied Blackie's lead to the leg of her desk.

"Right," Jean said, gazing down at Blackie over the top of her glasses. She waggled her finger. "Now, you behave yourself, please!"

Blackie barked and tried to jump up on Jean's lap. Mandy and James left her laughing and trying to make the puppy sit.

"Why have you brought Tinker back?" James asked curiously, as they settled the little cat back into one of the cages.

Mandy explained everything to him. "But I've got a feeling Dad's up to something," she said. "When I asked him, though, he just told me to wait and see."

"That's odd," James said. "I wonder what it can be."

Tinker looked pleased to be back at the surgery and quickly settled down on the blanket. "She seems to think this is her home," Mandy said with a sigh.

They didn't have to wait long to find out

what Mr Hope had been up to. A couple of minutes later he poked his head round the waiting-room door, where Mandy and James were trying to untangle Blackie's lead from the leg of Jean's desk.

"I've got some good news," Mr Hope said, a big grin on his face. "Miss Oswald is going to have Tinker after all!"

"Oh, Dad!" Mandy cried. "That's *brilliant*! But how? Has she found someone to look after her during the day?"

"Yes," her dad replied. "Us."

Mandy looked puzzled. "Us?"

"That's right," her dad confirmed. "I thought that if we offered to look after Tinker while Miss Oswald was at school, then she might be happy to give her a home. Once school breaks up for Christmas, there won't be a problem, and by the time the new term starts Tinker should have settled down in her new home. That will mean she'll be perfectly OK left on her own during the day."

Mandy threw her arms round her dad's waist. "Oh, Dad, that's *great*! Isn't it, James?"

"Brilliant," James said, grinning. "Totally."

"Isn't that the best news, Jean?" Mandy said.

Jean Knox nodded and smiled. "It certainly is," she said. "That sweet little cat really deserves a loving home."

"So when is Miss Oswald coming to pick her up?" James asked.

"Now," Mr Hope told him.

"Now!" Mandy shrieked. "Come on, James, let's get her ready." She dashed back into the residential unit, leaving James still trying to untangle Blackie's lead.

"She *is* ready. You got her ready this morning . . ." Mr Hope began, but Mandy had already taken Tinker from her cage and had started grooming her again. Tinker sat quietly on her lap looking very pleased, as if she knew something good was about to happen.

"I'm sure she knows," Mandy chuckled, as she gave the little cat a gentle hug. She sat back and gazed at Tinker's shining black fur. "There – you look very smart. You're the best possible Christmas present Miss Oswald could ever have."

"It's a bit early," James commented. He had given up trying to untangle Blackie and had followed Mandy through to the residential unit instead.

Mandy laughed. "Never mind," she said.

James looked out of the window. "Here's Miss Oswald now," he called as a car came to a halt on the gravel outside. The teacher jumped out and ran up the path.

"That was quick!" Mr Hope laughed, as Miss Oswald hurtled in through the door from the waiting-room. She scooped Tinker up off the worktop and hugged her close.

"Oh, Mr Hope!" she cried, her eyes shining. "I'm so pleased we've worked things out. I've been so worried about Tinker, and now everything has turned out well." She gave Tinker another hug. "Thank you so much!"

Mr Hope lent Miss Oswald a pet carrier and soon Tinker was settled into the back of her car. "I'll drop her off first thing Monday morning, then, if that's all right?" she said.

"Yes, that's fine," Mr Hope confirmed.

"I'll look after her until you pick her up," Mandy offered.

Miss Oswald smiled and gave her a hug. "Thank you, Mandy. I might be late some evenings, as there's so much work to do on the nativity play and pageant. But I know she'll be in safe hands here."

"I don't mind how late you are," Mandy said with a grin. "It'll be great having Tinker here. It will be like having our very own cat."

"So it will," Mr Hope said, as Miss Oswald got into her car and drove off down the lane. He glanced at his watch. "Well, I've got some farm visits to do. See you later, you two."

When they had finally untangled Blackie from the desk, Mandy and James set off down the lane with him towards the high street.

Mandy told James about seeing Gran outside Bleakfell Hall. "I'm dying to see what she's found," she said. "Let's call in on the way back from our walk."

Although there hadn't been any more snow, the trees in Monkton Spinney were white with frost. Blackie had a whale of a time shoving his

54

nose into the crunchy piles of frozen leaves that lay everywhere. He was having such fun that it took Mandy and James ages to persuade him that it was time to go home.

"Come on, Blackie!" Mandy called, still laughing at his antics. "We're going to Gran's. I'm sure she'll find you a biscuit if you're good."

At the word "biscuit", Blackie pricked up his ears and stayed still just long enough for James to clip on his lead.

The puppy pulled eagerly as they left the wood and made their way back over the bridge, then along the high street towards Lilac Cottage.

Gran had a great heap of clothes piled up on the kitchen table. She was busy sorting through them when Mandy and James appeared.

Their cheeks were red with cold after their walk in the biting wind. Blackie dragged James through the door. Then he headed straight for Gran's stove, where he sat warming himself.

"Hello, you three. How nice to see you. What have you been up to?" Gran asked.

Mandy quickly told her about Tinker.

"That's wonderful news." Gran beamed. "I've always thought Miss Oswald must be lonely in that house all on her own. Now she's got a pet to keep her company, so everything's worked out for the best."

"And, until the end of term, I get to look after Tinker before and after school!" Mandy said. "Isn't that great?"

"It certainly is," her gran agreed. "Now, help yourself to cookies." She put the tin in front of them. Then she noticed Blackie was sitting beside James with a hopeful look on his face. "Yes, Blackie, and you can have one of your *special* biscuits."

Gran took a packet from the cupboard and gave Blackie a large bone-shaped dog biscuit. She was very fond of James's puppy and always had a treat waiting when they brought him to visit her. Then she smiled at Mandy and James. "I'll make you a mug of hot chocolate when I've finished sorting through these clothes."

"Are you sorting stuff out for a jumble sale?" James asked.

Gran laughed. "No, these are the WI drama costumes. They have to be cleaned and pressed before our next production." She held up a long dress of pink silky material. "We don't really need this one any more. If I cut it down a bit, it will be just right for your pageant, Mandy. What do you think?"

Mandy took the dress from her gran and held it up against her. It was much too wide, and so long that it dragged on the floor. "But won't it need masses of work doing to it?" she asked doubtfully.

"That's no problem," Gran said as she bustled about making their hot chocolate.

Mandy still wasn't sure. The dress was *enormous*. She didn't think even Gran could make it fit her.

"Don't you worry, now, lass," said Mandy's grandad as he came in from the garden. He must have read the expression on her face. "Your gran can work miracles with that sewing-machine of hers. By the time she's finished, you'll have a dress fit for a princess, just you wait and see."

"Right, Mandy." Gran put two mugs of steaming hot chocolate down on the table, then she pulled out a chair. "Stand on this, please," she ordered.

Mandy clambered up on to the chair and stood there waiting while Gran fetched her sewing-box from the front room. She opened it up and took out a tape measure. Then, with a frown of concentration, she swiftly measured Mandy from neck to toe, across her back and chest and then down her arms. "Right," she

said. "That's all. Down you get, please. I'll get cracking this evening."

"Oh, Gran, you're so clever," Mandy said, giving her a quick hug. "Now all we need is James's short trousers."

Gran nodded mysteriously. "Don't worry, James, I've almost got that sorted out, as well."

"Oh?" James's mouth was full of walnut cookie. "That will be great – I think."

Gran laughed and patted him on the back. "Don't you fret, James. You *will* look really good in short trousers."

When Monday morning came, Miss Oswald dropped Tinker off at the cottage before school. It had started snowing and she had a few flakes stuck to her coat and scarf.

Mandy took the pet carrier from her. "Did she settle down all right?" she asked.

"Oh, yes." Miss Oswald smiled. "But she insisted on sleeping under my bed all night. I was going to get her a cat basket on Saturday, but the shops were closed by the time I'd settled her in. I'll get her one as soon as I can."

"That'll be nice," Mandy said.

"We'll put her in the cage for a while," said Mrs Hope when Miss Oswald had gone. "Then we'll gradually leave the door open, so she can come and go as she pleases. That way she'll feel more secure. Most animals like their own special bed to go to when they want to, so it will be good when Miss Oswald buys her a basket of her own."

Mandy's mum went into the residential unit and came back with one of the cages. She put it on the floor by the kitchen stove.

Mandy helped Tinker settle in. "There," she said gently. 'You'll be nice and warm. Now, be good," she added as she went to fetch her coat and hat. "I'll see you later."

By the time they were ready to leave, it was snowing hard. Mandy's mum dropped her off at the school gates – she and Gran were going Christmas shopping in Walton, their nearest town.

"Have fun," Mandy said, as she got out of the car.

"You too," Mrs Hope replied, waving goodbye.

Monday was the day of the pet auditions and Mandy had been talking about them all weekend. Lots of people were turning up outside the school with their cats, rabbits, guinea-pigs and hamsters, all safely tucked inside cosy baskets and boxes.

Mandy spotted Rachel Lowe coming along the street with Maisie, her lurcher. Maisie was wearing a cute sheepskin coat to keep out the cold. She also saw Sarah Drummond getting out of her mum's car with her puppy, Sooty. Sooty was Blackie's brother and the two puppies loved playing together.

Then Mandy saw Blackie. He was dragging James along the road towards the school gates. A shower of snow flew upwards as Blackie spotted Sooty, then lunged forward. *Uh-oh*, Mandy thought, chuckling to herself. *Here comes trouble!*

"He's going mad!" James panted, when he and Blackie reached her. His glasses were all crooked and his school-bag had toppled to one side. "He knows something's up. You can't keep anything secret from this puppy."

Mandy tried not to laugh as she helped James to straighten his bag. "Sit!" she said firmly to Blackie.

Blackie ignored her and barked at Sooty as if to say "Hello". Then he lunged towards Peter Foster, who was just coming through the school gates with his Cairn terrier, Timmy. James slipped and went flying, landing face down in a pile of soft snow. When he sat up, his face was red and his glasses had fallen off. "*Blackie!*" he shouted. "Sit!"

As Mandy helped James to recover his spectacles, she had a sneaky feeling that this was definitely *not* going to be one of Blackie's best-behaved days.

5

Good as gold

Mrs Garvie was just coming through the gate.
"James?" she said, when she saw him sitting in
the snow and Mandy trying to help him up.
"Did you slip over?"

"Er . . . yes." James brushed snow from his
coat and trousers.

"Are you hurt?" the teacher asked.

"No, I'm fine, thank you, Mrs Garvie," James assured her. He cleaned his glasses on his sleeve and shoved them back on.

"I take it Blackie has come for an audition?" Mrs Garvie stared at the puppy sternly.

"Er . . . yes," James admitted.

Mrs Garvie raised her eyebrows and went back into school without saying anything else.

Mandy could see James was upset that Blackie was being naughty already. "Don't worry." She tried to cheer him up. "He'll be all right – honestly, he will."

The pet auditions were to be held first thing, so parents could come to take the pets home at breaktime. Mandy and several of her friends had been given the job of painting the background scenery for the "Christmas Through the Ages" parade. This meant she would be in the school hall while the auditions were taking place.

People were already filing into the hall. When Mandy had found her painting apron, she hurried in after them.

Miss Oswald spotted her and came over. "Did Tinker settle in all right?" she asked anxiously.

"Yes, she was absolutely fine," Mandy assured her.

"That's good. Thank you, Mandy." The teacher smiled gratefully and hurried off to organise the pets and their owners.

Mrs Todd was waiting with the boxes of paints and brushes. She had sketched out several houses from different stages of history, so they would fit in with the children's costumes. There was a medieval wooden house, a farmhouse, a little stone cottage and a big Victorian mansion. Mandy and her friends were allowed to paint them in any colour they wanted.

"Now, you've got a lot to do," Mrs Todd reminded them. "So I want you to settle down to it as quickly as you can. I'll come back later to see how you are getting on."

Mandy dipped her brush in the brown paint pot and started to paint the walls of the medieval hut. Behind her in the hall, she could hear barks and miaows, and the *squeak, squeak* of guinea-pigs. She couldn't resist turning round to take a look at what was going on. There were owners and pets running all over the place.

Miss Oswald was standing by the stage holding a clipboard and looking flustered. "All right, Peter,' she called loudly. "You can lead Timmy on now!"

There was a scuffle from behind the curtains, then Peter Foster appeared. He was pulling at

a dog lead, but there didn't seem to be a dog at the end of it. Suddenly Timmy's brown nose and face peeped from behind the curtain. The little dog clearly didn't want to come on to the stage at all. He dug his claws into the floorboards and refused to budge.

Miss Oswald sighed. "OK, Peter, leave him for now. We'll try again later."

Peter went back behind the curtain and Mandy could hear him gently scolding Timmy.

Then Ross Jarvis appeared with his black-haired guinea-pig called Micky.

"Er . . . I don't think you should put him down on the floor," Miss Oswald called anxiously. "I don't think dogs and guinea-pigs mix very well."

Ross tucked Micky under his arm and walked across the stage. The guinea-pig's bright eyes looked around inquisitively and he gave a loud squeak before trying to tunnel his way up the sleeve of Ross's sweatshirt.

Everyone giggled as Ross left the stage with half a guinea-pig sticking out of his sleeve.

"Thank you, Ross. He'll be fine for the

pageant," Miss Oswald said. Then she consulted her list. "Next, please – Richard Tanner and Duchess."

"*Mandy!*" Mrs Todd's voice echoed across the hall. "You don't seem to have done very much!" She had come in and seen that Mandy was watching the auditions instead of getting on with painting.

"Oh, sorry, Mrs Todd," Mandy said, going a bit red. "I was just seeing how the pets were getting on. I wish I had a pet of my own to bring."

Mrs Todd smiled. "I know, Mandy. After all, having real pets *was* your idea. But we really need this scenery finished soon."

Mandy turned back quickly. In no time at all she had finished the front of the hut. She washed her brush, then dipped it in the yellow pot to paint the thatched roof. As she bent down, Blackie suddenly came hurtling towards her.

"Blackie!" James yelled frantically. But it was too late.

The puppy seemed determined to play with

Mandy, and not even James was going to stop him. He reached Mandy and jumped up, knocking both her and the yellow paint pot flying.

Mandy landed in a heap, yellow paint splattered all over her apron. "Oh, Blackie," Mandy said, but she couldn't help giggling.

The puppy jumped on top of her and licked her face all over. He had a big blob of yellow poster paint on his ear and looked so funny that by now everyone was laughing – even Miss Oswald and Mrs Todd.

"Oh, dear," Miss Oswald said, wiping her eyes. "Go and get him, James. And please try to keep him under control."

James pulled Blackie away from Mandy. "Sorry, Miss Oswald," he said sheepishly. "It's just that Mandy's his second-best friend, after me." He took Blackie off to the cloakroom to clean him up. When he came back, it was their turn for an audition.

"Round the hall, then up on the stage, please," Miss Oswald called.

Mandy held her breath. Would Blackie

behave himself or not? James would be so disappointed if his puppy let him down.

But she need not have worried. For once, Blackie was as good as gold. He trotted obediently by James's side as he walked round the hall and up the stairs on to the stage.

"Sit!" James commanded and, to Mandy's surprise, Blackie sat quietly down at James's feet and didn't move.

Miss Oswald clapped her hands. "Well done, James and Blackie," she called. "That was really excellent. Blackie has passed his audition with flying colours."

James beamed across at Mandy and did a thumbs-up sign. Mandy grinned and waved, heaving a sigh of relief.

Soon all the auditions were finished. They had all been very successful. The guinea-pigs had behaved well and so had the rabbits and cats. Timmy the terrier had at last decided he *would* walk across the stage. Sooty, who had obeyed Susan during his audition, was curled up now, fast asleep in the corner.

"Thank you so much all of you," Miss

71

Oswald called, as she ticked the last name off her list. "I'm pleased to tell you that *everyone* has passed."

Everyone cheered and clapped and all the dogs joined in, barking excitedly. Miss Oswald couldn't help laughing. "I hope they all behave as well on the day," she added. She turned to Mandy. "And thank *you*, Mandy, for suggesting we have real pets in the show. It is really going to be the best pageant ever."

Mandy felt herself blush with pleasure as everyone turned to look at her.

"Now," Miss Oswald continued, "don't forget it's the dress rehearsal on Thursday. You need to bring your costumes – but not your pets. I think it will be enough for their *owners* to know what to do – and the less excited they get, the better. "Oh . . ." she added, "I really need someone to help out with the animals during the pageant. Any volunteers?"

Hands flew up quickly, but Mandy's had shot up first.

"Right," Miss Oswald said. "Mandy, it would be lovely if you could help. I *know* you're good with pets." She pointed to Paul Stevens. "And you, Paul. I know you would have liked to bring Paddy if he hadn't been quite so big. You can help too." Paul had been disappointed because he hadn't been allowed to bring his pony along to the auditions.

Mandy was thrilled. Not only was she excited about being in the pageant, but now she was also going to help with the animals. She turned to James, who was standing nearby. "Wait until I tell Mum and Dad *this*!" she said excitedly.

Before they all filed out to their parents, who were waiting to collect the pets, Miss Oswald had a request to make. "I wonder if any of you have an old doll's cradle we could disguise as a manger?" she asked everyone. "I thought I'd got everything organised," she confessed. "But I seem to have forgotten one of the most important things."

Again, Mandy's hand shot up first. Somewhere at the back of her toy cupboard she had a cradle, along with lots of other things she didn't play with any more. "I've got one,

Miss Oswald," she called. "You're welcome to borrow it."

"Oh, thank you, Mandy," Miss Oswald looked relieved. "Could I pick it up later, when I come to collect Tinker?"

"Yes, that'll be fine," Mandy said.

As usual, Mandy couldn't wait to get home at the end of the afternoon to tell her parents all the day's news. James had already arranged with his mum that he would have tea at Animal Ark so he could see Tinker before she went home.

When they arrived, they found Mandy's mum and gran sitting at the table drinking cups of tea. They both looked tired out. There was a big pile of plastic carrier bags under the table. As Mandy and James came in, Mrs Hope quickly gathered them up and disappeared upstairs.

"Presents," James whispered in Mandy's ear.

"Hope so," she whispered back.

"I've got a surprise for you," Gran said, pointing to one of the chairs. Draped over

74

the back was the Victorian dress.

Mandy gasped as she held it up against her. It seemed to have shrunk miraculously to Mandy's size. "Wow, Gran, it's great. Thank you!"

"I hope it fits," Gran said.

"Why don't you run upstairs and try it on?" her mum suggested, as she came back into the kitchen.

Gran picked up a brown paper parcel from the table and handed it to James. "And this is for *you*, James."

James tore off the paper eagerly. Inside was a pair of grey short trousers and a pair of long woollen socks.

"A friend of mine gave them to me," Gran explained. "And your mum called me today to say that someone has given her a Fair Isle jumper for you."

James didn't say anything at first. He was staring at the short trousers with a worried look on his face.

"What do you think of them?" Mandy asked, still holding her dress up against her.

James swallowed. "Er . . . I'm not sure what they'll look like when I've got them on."

Gran and Mrs Hope laughed. "Don't worry, James," Mrs Hope said quickly. "They'll look great — honestly."

James wrapped the clothes up again. "Hope so," he said dubiously.

"But what about the gas mask?" Mandy asked suddenly.

Gran looked thoughtful. "We'll have to wait and see. I've asked Grandad to see if one of his old village friends knows where we could get one."

Mandy went upstairs to try on her dress. She looked at herself in the full-length mirror on the landing. It fitted beautifully. Gran had also made some petticoats to go underneath, which made the frills stand out.

"Wow!" James said when she came back downstairs to show everyone. "You look brilliant."

"It's lovely, Mandy," her mum said. "A proper Victorian young lady."

"I wouldn't like to have to wear it all the

time, though," Mandy said. "It wouldn't be very easy to have snowball fights in!"

Everyone laughed. "No, you're right," Gran said. "It's really more of a party dress."

When Mandy had changed back into her jeans and trainers, she and James told Gran and Mrs Hope all about the pet auditions. They laughed when they heard about Blackie and the paint pot.

"I'm really looking forward to the pageant," Mrs Hope said, wiping her eyes.

"Me too," Gran agreed.

Then Mandy remembered her promise to Miss Oswald. "I've got to sort out my toy cupboard before Miss Oswald comes," she told them. "I said she could borrow my old doll's cradle, to use as a manger in the nativity play."

"While you're about it, Mandy," Mrs Hope suggested, "perhaps you could sort out some of the other toys. We can take them to the cottage hospital for the children's ward."

"That's a great idea," Mandy said. "I'll do it as soon as we've said hello to Tinker."

"She's in the study with Dad at the moment," Mrs Hope told her.

Mandy and James left Gran and Mrs Hope to finish their tea and they hurried into the study. Tinker was sitting on the big old desk, watching Mr Hope fill in some forms.

Mandy picked her up, then sat on a chair with the cat on her lap. "She looks great, doesn't she?" she said to her dad.

"Yes," Mr Hope replied. "She's a lot better."

"Can we take her up to my room?" Mandy asked.

"I don't see why not," her dad said. "You'd better ask Mum if it's all right, though."

Mandy handed Tinker to James so he could carry her through into the kitchen.

"Of course it's all right," Mrs Hope said when they asked. "She can help you sort out your toy cupboard."

Upstairs, James put Tinker on the bed and stroked her while Mandy looked in her toy cupboard. It was chock-a-block with soft toys, jigsaw puzzles, games and dolls. Mandy pulled them out one by one. Right at the back was the wooden doll's cradle. She hauled it out and gave it a quick dust down.

"This will be all right, won't it?" she asked James.

"Looks fine to me," James replied.

Mandy sorted through the toys, putting the broken ones to one side. Soon there was a large pile of good toys on the floor beside the bed, ready to go to the children's ward. She sat back on her heels. "*Now* there's room for my *new* Christmas presents," she said to James with a grin.

Mrs Hope popped her head round the door. "Miss Oswald's here for Tinker," she said. She gazed at the pile of toys and games. "Good job, Mandy. I'll drop them off at the hospital next time I'm passing," she offered. "I'm sure they'll be very pleased to have them."

"Thanks, Mum," Mandy said. She picked up the cradle and carried it downstairs. James followed with Tinker in his arms.

As soon as the little cat heard Miss Oswald's voice, she pricked up her ears and struggled to get down. When James put her on the floor she scampered into the kitchen, where her owner was waiting. The teacher scooped her up in her arms and gave her a hug. Miss Oswald's serious face softened as she laid her cheek against Tinker's fur.

When Miss Oswald had finished fussing her cat, she noticed the cradle Mandy was carrying. "Oh, thank you!" she exclaimed. "That's perfect."

6

Dress rehearsal

On Thursday, Miss Oswald arrived with
Tinker at eight in the morning. "I hope you
don't mind me being so early," she said quickly
as she handed the little cat over to Mandy at
the front door. "But there's so much to do at
school today I thought I'd better get there as
soon as I could. I even had to wake poor

81

Tinker up," she added. "She was fast asleep."

"I'm sure she didn't mind," Mandy said, pleased to have an extra half-hour with the little cat before she left for school herself.

After Miss Oswald had gone, Mandy took Tinker out of her carrier. The little cat went over to the stove and sat by it, then began washing her face with her paws. Mandy went back to the table to finish her cereal.

After a while, Tinker came over and jumped on her lap, purring.

"Sorry, Tinker." Mandy put her gently back on to the floor. "I'd love to stay here with you, but there's lots to do today."

She was just washing up her bowl when the phone rang. Mandy's mum was out on a call and her dad was getting ready for morning surgery, so Mandy went to answer it. Tinker followed her out into the hall.

It was Gran, sounding very pleased about something. "I was at a WI meeting last night, Mandy. And a friend of mine said she'd seen *two* gas masks in a junk shop in Walton."

"Two!" Mandy said.

"Yes," Gran went on. "I'm taking Grandad Christmas shopping tomorrow, so we'll ask the woman in the shop if we can borrow them for the pageant. One of my friends knows her, and says she's sure the lady will let us."

"That would be brilliant, Gran," Mandy said. "James will be ever so pleased."

"It was rather late when I got home yesterday evening so I tried to phone James's mum this morning to tell her, but I haven't managed to get hold of her yet," Gran went on.

Mandy glanced at the clock on the wall. "Maybe she's driven James to school today," she said. "I'll tell him when I get there, OK?"

"Thank you, Mandy," Gran said. "If you call in after school, I'm sure we'll be back from Walton by then."

"Thanks, Gran," Mandy said. "It's the dress rehearsal for the nativity and pageant today," she added excitedly.

"Dress rehearsal!" Gran said. "Well, good luck, love. I'm sure it will go well. I hope the frock will be all right."

"It's going to be brilliant, Gran," Mandy said. "Everyone's dying to see it."

"See you later, then," Gran said, hanging up.

Tinker followed Mandy back into the kitchen. She settled down by the stove again as Mandy got her things ready for school. Her dress was carefully packed in tissue paper in a carrier bag.

Mandy's mum got back from her morning visit just as she was leaving. "Good luck with the rehearsal, love," she said, kissing Mandy goodbye.

Mandy hurried along the lane and down the street towards school. The sky was grey and it looked like more snow was on its way. Yesterday's fall still lay in a crunchy, sparkly coating on the ground.

Passing the village green, Mandy noticed that a huge Christmas tree had been put up in the middle of it. Every Christmas Eve the WI choir and villagers gathered round the tree to sing carols and eat hot roasted chestnuts. Mandy shivered with excitement. She loved it when the whole village gathered together like that.

All the shop windows were decorated with Christmas lights. They sparkled in the winter morning gloom as Mandy hurried by.

James was waiting for her by the school gate. He looked pleased when she told him about the gas mask. "My costume looked brilliant," he said with a grin. "Even if Dad did say the trousers showed my knobbly knees . . ."

"They would have been *frozen* knobbly knees if boys had to wear them in this cold weather," Mandy said laughing.

A few minutes later, they were in their

separate classrooms and getting changed for the dress rehearsal. Miss Oswald was leading the infants into the hall to rehearse their nativity play and Mandy watched from her classroom as they all filed past in their costumes. She counted three shepherds, the Three Wise Men, lots of angels and sheep, and a couple of donkeys. This made Mandy smile – she remembered wearing the donkey costume herself when she was an infant. Last of all, Libby Masters passed by dressed as Mary, with one of the boys from her class, who was dressed as Joseph.

Mandy ran to help as Joseph almost tripped over the long, stripy curtain he was wearing as a tunic. "Watch out," she said, tying the dressing-gown cord around his waist more securely. "There, you should be all right now."

Mandy watched Joseph hurry after Libby into the school hall. She thought the infants looked great in their costumes.

When all of Mandy's class were dressed and ready for the pageant, they waited in the corridor outside the hall.

Mandy peeped in through the crack between the double doors. The cloth with the painted houses on had been draped down the side of the hall. On the stage Miss Oswald had covered Mandy's old doll's cradle in a white cloth and filled it with hay. It looked just like a manger.

Class 4 had made a huge gold star, which hung from the ceiling at the back of the stage. The angels, who were all dressed in white sheets with golden cardboard wings, were standing underneath it.

The Three Wise Men arrived with their gifts and Mandy could hear them saying their lines. "We saw a bright star in the east," one of them said. "And we followed it here to the stable," another continued.

The dress rehearsal for the nativity seemed to be going perfectly. Mandy hoped the rehearsal for the pageant would go just as well.

As soon as the infants had finished, the juniors went into the hall and lined up for their parade.

Miss Oswald smiled, then she turned to everyone. "Now, you'll all be coming in at the back of the hall," she called. "You and your pets will walk down either side of the hall, in front of the painted houses and along the front of the stage. Meanwhile, Mrs Garvie will be telling everyone about Christmas celebrations throughout history." She looked around. "We'll just go through that, shall we?"

When everybody had practised several times, Miss Oswald went up on to the stage. "Right, everyone. Now remember – after the 'Christmas Through the Ages' parade, all of you in costume will come up here to gather round the manger. This will bring together all the different generations that have celebrated Christmas over the years – from the very first Christmas with the Wise Men bringing their gifts, right up to the present day."

James was standing next to Mandy. "It's going to be great, isn't it?" he whispered.

"Brilliant," she whispered. Her heart turned over with excitement. This year's Christmas show really was going to be the best ever.

The dress rehearsal was soon over and Miss Oswald seemed really pleased with everyone. "If you do it as well tomorrow," she said, "I shall be very proud of you all. And your pets, of course."

After school, Mandy and James went straight to Lilac Cottage to see if Gran and Grandad had managed to borrow the gas masks.

"There you are," Grandad said, grinning as they came in. "Gas masks." He pointed to two small leather boxes with straps on the kitchen table. He undid the catch on one of the boxes and took out a strange-looking object. It was like a helmet, but made of rubber, and had a round metal disc with a hole in the front to go over the nose and plastic goggles to go over the eyes. "My, my," he said, "this takes me back a bit."

James pulled a face. "I haven't got to *wear* it, have I? I'll look like a monster from outer space, instead of a boy from the second world war."

Grandad burst out laughing. "Goodness me, no. You just carry the box in case of an attack."

"Oh." James looked relieved. "That's all right, then."

"The woman in the shop lent us both of

them," Gran said. "So we thought perhaps Blackie might like to carry one round his neck, too."

Mandy and James laughed at the idea of Blackie carrying a gas mask. "Oh, Grandad!" Mandy chuckled. "I'm sure he'll love to."

It was almost dark when Mandy and James said goodbye and hurried off in their opposite directions home. Flakes of snow were fluttering in the air as Mandy hurried up her front path and round to the back door. Standing by the step was her dad, admiring a shiny green Christmas tree in a tub.

"Good, huh?" he said to Mandy.

She clapped her hands in delight. One of the best Christmas things of all was decorating the tree. "It's lovely! Did you get it from Mr Fenton?" she asked her dad, giving him a big smile. Amy Fenton was one of Mandy's school-friends. Her dad worked at the sawmills where they sold fir-trees at Christmas-time.

"That's right," Mr Hope confirmed. "He delivered it this afternoon. Come on – let's get it inside before your mum gets home. It'll be a nice surprise for her."

With a lot of pushing and pulling, they finally managed to get the tree through the kitchen and into the sitting-room. Adam Hope set it down in the corner by the fireplace. The wide fragrant branches touched the walls either side. There was just enough room to put the golden star on top.

Mandy sniffed in the sharp, pine smell of the branches. She had forgotten how wonderful

91

Christmas trees smelled. "When can we decorate it?" she asked excitedly.

Her dad laughed. "How about after evening surgery? You know your mum likes us all to do it together."

Mandy nodded happily, then went off to find Tinker.

She soon found the little cat curled up contentedly on her bed. Tinker obviously hadn't been disturbed by all the noise they'd been making. It was good to know she was becoming less nervous and jumpy.

Mandy picked Tinker up and took her downstairs to show her the tree. "Do you like it?" she asked the little cat.

Tinker purred.

Mandy laughed. "Tinker likes the tree," she said to her dad, as he came in with a huge cardboard box full of decorations. He set it down on the floor. "There you are," he said. "Why don't you sort these out, ready for when Mum gets in."

Mandy sat on the floor sorting out the decorations. There were glass baubles, tinsel, stars, tiny Father Christmases, and a whole string of fairy lights.

Tinker, her green eyes bright with curiosity, patted the shiny baubles with her soft paws as Mandy took each one out of the box. Mandy laughed, hugging the little cat.

When Miss Oswald arrived to collect Tinker, Mandy took her into the sitting-room.

Tinker was curled up underneath the Christmas tree, fast asleep. She opened an eye when Mandy and Miss Oswald came into the room, and immediately got up to greet her owner, her tail waving in the air.

"I tried to get her a basket in Walton," the teacher told Mandy as she stroked her pet. "But the pet shop had sold out."

"Sold out!" Mandy said. "I suppose lots of people have been buying new things for their pets."

Miss Oswald nodded. "I'm so late doing my shopping that lots of things have already gone. But the owner said he'd be getting some more in after Christmas," she went on. "I'm afraid

Tinker will have to wait until then."

It was only just getting light the following morning when Mandy got up, and it was snowing heavily. She felt a tingle of happiness when she passed the sitting-room on her way to the kitchen. The Christmas tree looked beautiful. Mandy and her parents had decorated it after evening surgery.

Mandy was just packing her bag for school when there was a knock at the door. She couldn't help laughing when her mum opened it. Miss Oswald stood there. She was already covered with snow, even though she had only walked from her car to the front door!

The teacher smiled, then handed the cat carrier over to Mrs Hope. "I'd best not come in today," she said. "The driving conditions are a bit difficult – as you can see! It will take me longer to get to school in all this snow, and there's lots to do!" She looked at Mandy. "If you don't mind getting to school a few minutes earlier than usual, Mandy, you're welcome to have a lift."

Mandy nodded. "Thanks, Miss Oswald." She smiled. "It'll save Mum getting the Land-rover out."

Mrs Hope nodded gratefully.

Rushing to pull on her coat, gloves and woolly hat, Mandy said a quick hello to Tinker along the way, then followed Miss Oswald to her car.

The teacher drove carefully down the lane. As she was about to pull out into the high street, a snowplough came trundling along. Its huge scrapers sent fountains of snow shooting out to the sides of the road as it went. Miss Oswald waited until the vehicle had passed by, then slowly made her way to school.

There weren't going to be any lessons that day. Instead, each class would play games and take it in turns to rehearse their parts in the show with Miss Oswald for the last time. Then there would be a special Christmas lunch-time, with balloons and party food, before parents started to arrive – some of them with pets that were going to be in the show!

★　★　★

After a fun morning and lunch-time, the whole school was humming with excitement.

Mandy's class had changed into their costumes and they all looked splendid. Gary Roberts was dressed in a brown tunic and leggings as a boy from medieval times, Pam Stanton wore a flowery peasant's dress. Richard Tanner was wearing flared purple trousers and an embroidered sheepskin waistcoat as a boy from the 1970s.

Looking through the classroom window, Mandy noticed that James's mum and dad had arrived and were leading Blackie through the school gates and into the playground. Mrs Hunter had Blackie's gas-mask box in her hand.

Mandy and Paul Stevens hurried along to Class 1, where all the pets and owners were gathering until it was time for the pageant. The tables and chairs had been pushed to one end of the room.

To Mandy's surprise, her mum was there. "Mum!" she exclaimed. "You should be in the hall; otherwise you won't get a seat."

"I've brought you a surprise," Mrs Hope said,

taking Tinker out of the pet carrier at her feet. Mandy could hardly believe her eyes. Then her mum handed her the little cat and said, "Miss Oswald thought a Victorian girl should have a little cat as a pet."

Mandy beamed as her mum explained that Miss Oswald had rung the surgery earlier on and asked Mrs Hope to bring Tinker along.

"Good luck, love." Mrs Hope smiled, then hurried off to take her place in the hall.

Everyone gathered round to say hello to Tinker. The little cat purred as lots of hands reached out to stroke her. But Mandy felt her flinch as Timmy the Cairn terrier barked loudly and Blackie barked back. Although Tinker had got to know Blackie, she was still nervous of strange dogs.

Some time later, Mrs Garvie came into the classroom. She warned everyone that the infants' nativity play had almost finished and it would soon be their turn to be on stage. Mandy took Tinker over to introduce her to the Headteacher and tell her the good news.

"That's wonderful, Mandy," Mrs Garvie said

with a smile. "But don't forget – I need you and Paul to help with the other animals as well."

"I won't," Mandy assured her quickly, popping Tinker back into her carrier. Then she grabbed the big bag of pet treats she'd brought with her, ready for later.

"Make sure your dogs and cats are safely on their leads," Mrs Garvie said to the children as she started to line them up in the corridor. "We don't want them to run off."

In the hall, the final scene of the nativity play was taking place. Mandy went on ahead and took a peep through the door. Mary and Joseph were sitting on bales of hay in the stable, surrounded by angels and the Three Wise Men.

Then Miss Oswald appeared and asked everyone to file quietly along the corridor and wait outside the hall doors. She would signal when it was time for them to go in.

Mandy came back and handed Paul the bag of pet treats. "Give a few of these to each owner," she suggested. "Then, if their pets get restless, the treats might keep them quiet for a few minutes."

"Good idea," Paul said. He went down the line handing out the treats.

Mandy ran back to the classroom to fetch Tinker. Her heart thumped with excitement. She knew her mum and dad, Gran and Grandad and lots of other friends from the village were all in the hall watching. She would feel so proud carrying Tinker in the parade. She just couldn't wait!

But when Mandy reached the classroom she gave a horrified gasp. The door of Tinker's cat carrier was open . . . and Tinker was gone!

7

A frantic search

Mandy searched under every table and chair, even in the cupboards, desperately calling Tinker's name. But it was no good; Tinker was nowhere in the room. She had completely disappeared.

Mandy was close to tears. What on earth should she do? It was nearly time for the pageant and she had to make sure all the other pets were settled and ready. How could she do that and hunt for Tinker at the same time? The little cat could be anywhere in the whole school by now.

Lifting her long skirt up to her knees, Mandy dashed out of the classroom and along the corridor. "Tinker! Good puss, where are you?" she called desperately. She ran into the cloakroom – no sign of her there, either. All the other classroom doors and Mrs Garvie's office door were closed, so Tinker couldn't be in any of those rooms.

Mandy gave a sigh of despair. Where else could she look? Then she saw James coming towards her with Blackie.

"Everyone's wondering where you'd got to," he told her.

"Tinker's gone!" she wailed.

"Oh, no!" James gasped. He looked thoughtful. "Maybe she's gone into the hall to find Miss Oswald," he said.

Mandy gazed at him. "Yes, she might have done. Let's go and look."

Outside the hall, Miss Oswald had come out to check that everyone was ready. "Mandy! James! What on earth are you doing?" she asked.

"I'm sorry, but I've lost Tinker," Mandy confessed tearfully.

"Oh dear," Miss Oswald said, looking worried. "I wonder what could have happened to her." Then her face cleared. "Try not to worry too much, Mandy. All the main doors to the school are shut, so she won't come to any harm. I think we'll just have to begin the pageant without her."

"Couldn't we just look in the hall?" Mandy pleaded.

"Well, OK, but be as quick as you can," Miss Oswald said. "The infants will get fidgety if there's too much of a delay."

James gave Blackie's lead to Paul, then followed Mandy into the hall.

"James, you go down to the front and I'll start at the back," Mandy said, getting on to her hands and knees and beginning to crawl in between the rows of seats.

"Right," James said looking a little uncertain.

As Mandy scrambled along the back row of the audience, her feet kept getting caught up in the frills of her dress, which slowed her down. *I don't suppose Victorian girls had to crawl around the floor very often*, she thought to herself.

"Sorry," she muttered as she trampled over someone's foot. "Er . . . excuse me," she apologised to a lady as she knocked over her handbag.

Then Mandy's hair ribbon came undone and

dangled across her eyes. She pushed it away, not stopping to pick it up when it fell on the floor. People shuffled up and down. One or two stood up to let her past, giving her strange looks as she looked underneath the seats. "Excuse me," she said again, trying to peer between the chairs and through people's legs. Then she came face to face with a pair of trousers and boots that she recognised.

"Mandy, what on *earth* are you doing?" her dad's voice hissed out from above her head.

Mandy sat up on her knees and brushed her hair out of her eyes. "I'm looking for Tinker," she said in a tearful voice.

"Tinker? Why, have you lost her?" her dad asked.

"Yes, I'm afraid so," Mandy admitted. Mr Hope stood up. "Has anyone seen a little black cat," he called. "She seems to have gone missing."

Everyone got to their feet and shuffled about, looking under their seats and shaking their heads. James crawled out from the middle row. His school cap was tipped over one eye, and the gas mask round his neck kept knocking into his chest.

By now Mandy's dress was covered in dust and grime. She tried to brush it off as she made her way back to the side of the hall. She knew she must look a mess.

When she and James went back outside the hall, Paul handed over Blackie's lead. Mrs Garvie then announced that the "Christmas Through the Ages" pageant was about to begin.

"Mandy and Paul, check that all the pets are ready, please," Miss Oswald said quickly. Then she disappeared into the hall to take her place by the stage.

Mandy and Paul went along the line, checking all the pets were settled and ready. Mandy gave Blackie a hug. "Now behave yourself, *please*, Blackie," she whispered in the puppy's ear. "Good luck!" she said to James, before she peered through the door, looking out for a sign from Miss Oswald. The teacher gave the signal and the pageant parade began.

"Christmas has been celebrated throughout

the ages in many different ways, although the message of goodwill and peace has been the same since the very start," Mrs Garvie said into the microphone.

"Oooh!" the audience said, as Sarah came in as a Roman peasant girl. She was dressed in a long brown tunic made of rough material, with a rope for a belt and sandals on her feet.

"Aah!" everyone exclaimed. "How sweet!" They clapped as Sooty bounced along beside Sarah, his tail waving in the air. He was behaving like a dream.

"In the early days," Mrs Garvie continued, "the Romans were persecuted for their Christian beliefs and had to celebrate in secret with a simple feast."

Mandy watched as each of her friends walked towards the stage with their pets. Soon it would be her turn. She looked up and saw her mum and dad, Gran and Grandad, all smiling proudly and nodding at her. She brushed the last bit of dust off her skirt and quickly ran her fingers through her hair.

Mandy's heart gave a thud of excitement as

her turn came to walk down the aisle to the front of the stage. She heard one lady admiring her dress, and the audience clapped loudly as she reached her place next to the others.

Mandy gave a sigh. She was really enjoying being part of the pageant, but still wondered where Tinker had got to.

Then it was James and Blackie's turn. The audience chuckled as James hung on to Blackie's lead tightly as the puppy suddenly spotted Sooty and tried to hurtle forward.

"Wait!" James commanded. He fished in his pocket for a treat. Blackie gobbled it up eagerly and stayed obediently beside James as he walked towards the stage. The audience clapped harder than ever.

"During the war," Mrs Garvie continued, "people had to celebrate Christmas as best they could. Food was rationed, and after dark no lights were allowed in houses, in case of enemy attack. But everyone managed to have a good time, and although the children didn't have many presents everybody still enjoyed the spirit of Christmas."

Suddenly, Blackie's ears shot up. He gave a yelp and frantically tried to climb on to the stage. Luckily, James managed to haul him back.

"Even dogs," Mrs Garvie added, and the audience laughed.

Peter Foster and Timmy were the last in the parade. Peter was dressed as a boy from the present day in a track suit and trainers. Timmy trotted down the aisle next to him and, to everyone's relief, was good as gold.

When all the pupils were assembled along the front of the hall, they split into two groups. Then they filed up on either side of the stage to gather round the manger to sing a Christmas carol.

Mandy took her place at the side of the stage. The music began and everyone started to sing "Away in a Manger".

When the carol had finished, the applause was deafening. The nativity and pageant had been an enormous success.

8

Surprise!

"Well done, everyone!" Miss Oswald said proudly, as she walked on to the side of the stage. "You didn't find Tinker, then?" she whispered to Mandy.

Mandy shook her head. "No, I'm sorry."

Miss Oswald patted her shoulder. "Never mind, Mandy, we'll have a proper search in a minute."

But suddenly, from the centre of the stage, there came a startled cry. It was Libby Masters. She was clutching the doll dressed as the baby Jesus, and looking frightened.

"Libby! What's wrong?" Miss Oswald asked urgently.

"There's something in the manger!" Libby shrieked.

"Oh, Libby, you're imagining things," Miss Oswald said.

Then everyone gasped as a small black head popped up, followed by a thin miaow. It was Tinker! The little cat peered round the stage, blinking at everyone with her big green eyes. Then she saw her owner, and with another miaow she leaped straight from the manger and into Miss Oswald's arms.

"Tinker!" Miss Oswald cried out. "There you are, Mandy," she said, laughing. "I didn't have to try to find Tinker, after all. She found me!" Everyone laughed and clapped as Miss Oswald held her little pet close and kissed her on the head. And Mandy's heart skipped with relief . . .

Afterwards, while everyone was changing out of their costumes, Miss Oswald came in with Tinker to explain what had happened. "Tinker's been sleeping in the cradle at home," she told everyone. "I haven't been able to buy her a proper cat basket yet, so she made up her mind that the doll's cradle would do for the time being. It's just the right size for her." The teacher chuckled.

"She must have made her way to the hall when she escaped from her basket, then spotted the cradle on stage." Mandy laughed. "She probably thought you had put it there just for her."

By now, everyone was crowding round Tinker and Miss Oswald. Blackie jumped up to give Tinker a friendly lick on the nose.

"No wonder Blackie tried to climb on to the stage," James said with a grin. "He knew Tinker was in the cradle and wanted to wake her up to play with him."

"Trust Blackie." Mandy laughed, bending down to give the puppy a hug.

Miss Oswald handed the little cat to Mandy. "Would you put her safely in her carrier until we're ready to go home?" she asked.

Mandy took the little cat gratefully. She was relieved that Miss Oswald trusted her to take care of Tinker again. "I'll make sure the door is shut properly this time," she assured her.

Miss Oswald smiled and gave Mandy a hug. "Don't worry about her escaping, Mandy. No harm has been done, and I think the excitement rather added to our Christmas pageant!"

Everyone agreed and Mandy felt much better.

As she helped to tidy up, Mandy had an idea. "Do you think Tinker would like the cradle as a Christmas present?" she asked James, who was tidying up with one hand and holding Blackie's lead with the other.

"I'm *sure* she would," James said. "Then Miss Oswald wouldn't need to buy a new basket."

"Right," Mandy said. "That's what I'll do, then."

When the stage had been cleared and everyone was getting ready to go home, Mandy collected Tinker and went off to find Miss Oswald.

She was saying goodbye to the last of the parents. Mr and Mrs Hope were waiting for Mandy by the doors with Gran and Grandad.

She told them her idea about the cradle.

Gran gave her a hug. "That *is* a brainwave," she said, as Miss Oswald came over.

"What is?" Miss Oswald asked, taking the pet carrier gently from Mandy. Tinker was peering out at her through the mesh.

"Do you think Tinker would like to keep the cradle as her Christmas present?" Mandy asked shyly.

Miss Oswald's face lit up. "Oh, Mandy, that is kind of you," she said. "I'm sure she would love it more than anything." She gazed at the cat. "Wouldn't you, Tinker?"

Tinker purred as if to show her approval.

"Well, that's settled." Mandy's dad chuckled. "She thinks it's a great idea."

Mandy said goodbye to everyone and made her way outside to the Land-rover with her parents. Miss Oswald followed with Tinker in

the carrier. It had stopped snowing and the whole of the village was covered in a thick layer of white. It sparkled like silver in the darkening sky.

Mandy drew in her breath. It looked just like a scene from a Christmas card. She bent down to say goodbye to Tinker. "Merry Christmas," she whispered to the little cat. "I hope I'll see you again soon."

"Of course you will," Miss Oswald said with a smile. "You can come and see her any time you wish." She put the cat carrier into the back of her car, then placed the cradle beside it. "I'm sure she's going to miss you."

"I'm going to miss her, as well," Mandy said. "I'll come over soon to make sure she likes her present."

"We'll look forward to seeing you," Miss Oswald said.

Mandy's heart sang with happiness as she climbed into the back of the Land-rover. Mr Hope started the engine and soon they were driving along the high street.

As the vehicle turned into the lane leading

to Animal Ark, Mandy could see the lights from their Christmas tree sparkling in the cottage window to welcome them home.

"Oh," Mandy sighed. "Doesn't the tree look lovely?"

"Beautiful," Mrs Hope said, and Mr Hope nodded in agreement.

"So *Christmassy*!" Mandy exclaimed. She leaned forward. "And Tinker looked so happy to be going home with Miss Oswald, didn't she?"

"She certainly did," Mrs Hope said, turning round to give Mandy a smile.

Mandy sat back with a sigh of satisfaction. It had been so nice looking after Tinker, she just couldn't wait to visit her in the holidays and see her curled up in her cradle.

There was no doubt about it – this really was going to be a lovely Christmas!

EMERALD, AMBER AND JET

Nine Lives 1

Lucy Daniels

Bracken, the Bradmans' cat, has given birth to nine adorable kittens. Nine very different personalities each need very special homes. Can the Bradmans be sure they've found the right owners?

Green-eyed Emerald wants to find out what her owner does at work, but her curiosity could lose him his job.

Amber is a gorgeous golden tabby – but she's convinced she's a dog! Will she discover the advantages of being a cat?

Jet is thrilled with his new home – he gets so much attention. But what will happen when another little visitor arrives?

GINGER, NUTMEG AND CLOVE
Nine Lives 2

Lucy Daniels

Bracken, the Bradmans' cat, has given birth to nine adorable kittens. Nine very different personalities each need very special homes. Can the Bradmans be sure they've found the right owners?

Red-haired Ginger is fearless and nosy – will he settle in with Amy and her mother, or will he be too much of a handful?

Long-haired Nutmeg is really naughty and her new owners don't know how to keep her out of trouble. Until one day Nutmeg's inquisitiveness teaches her a lesson . . .

Clove isn't very happy in her new home and won't eat the food Mr Miller gives her. Then the most unexpected person comes up with the answer.

DAISY, BUTTERCUP AND WEED

Nine Lives 3

Lucy Daniels

Bracken, the Bradmans' cat, has given birth to nine adorable kittens. Nine very different personalities each need very special homes. Can the Bradmans be sure they've found the right owners?

Snow-white Daisy is adorable – but very *very* quiet. What will make Daisy miaow for the first time?

Everyone wants to play with Buttercup. But can she please everybody at once?

Scrawny little Weed is the runt of the litter – who will want her? The Bradmans despair . . . but the answer is close at hand.